Melting Ice Cubes

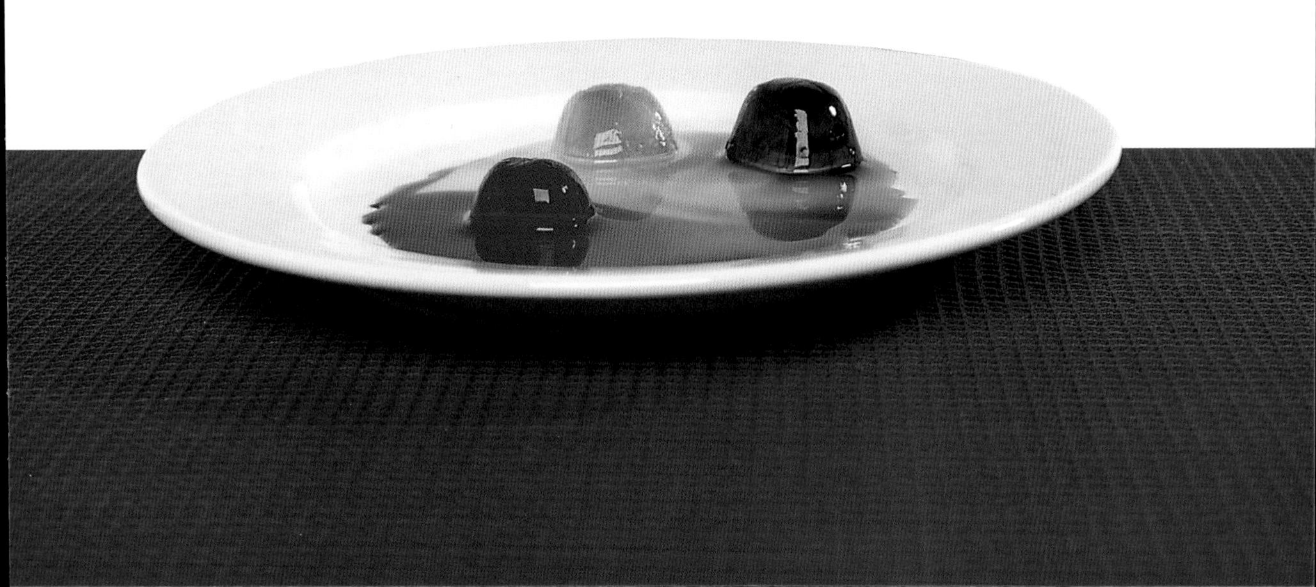

Here is a red ice cube.

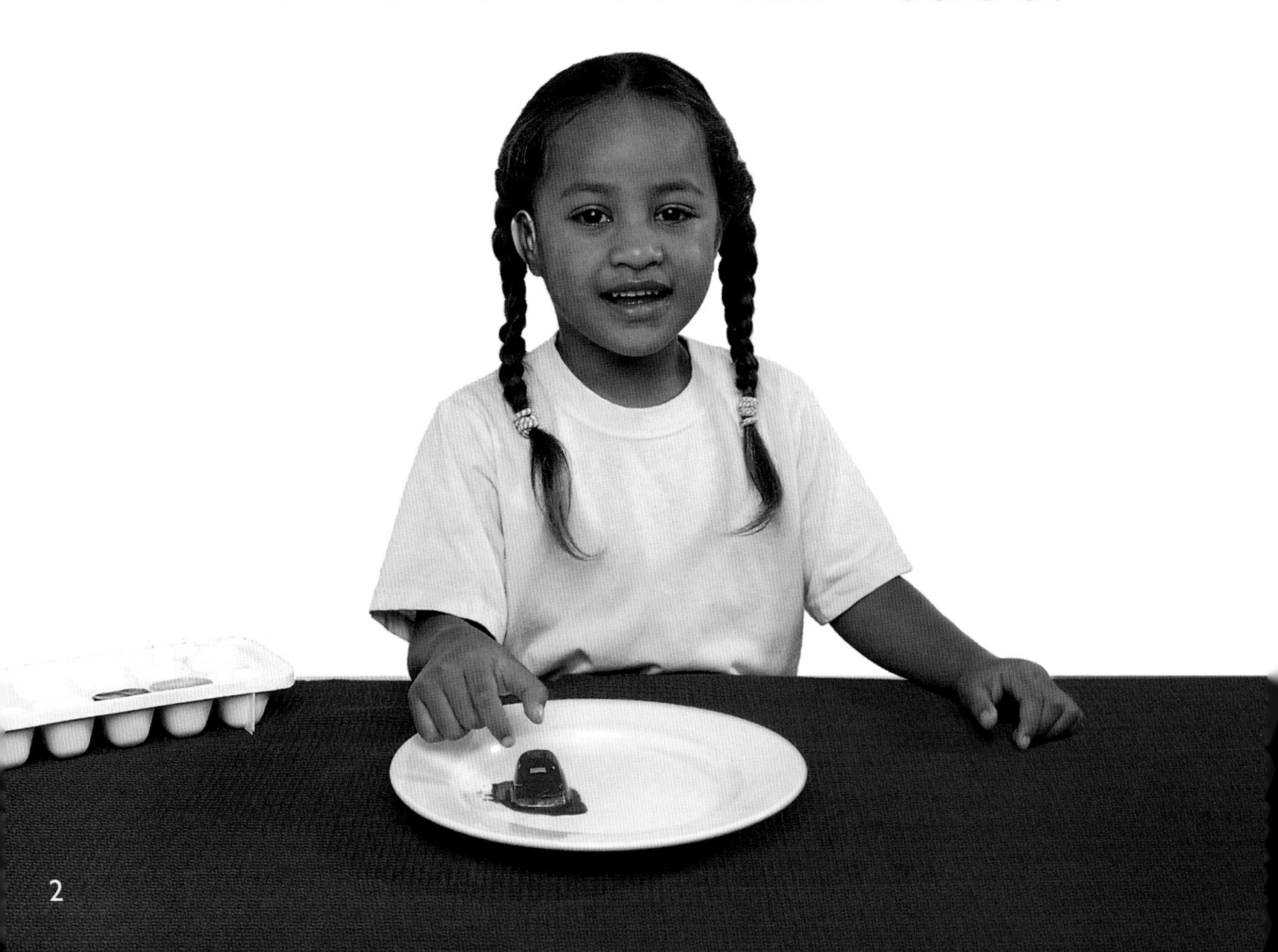

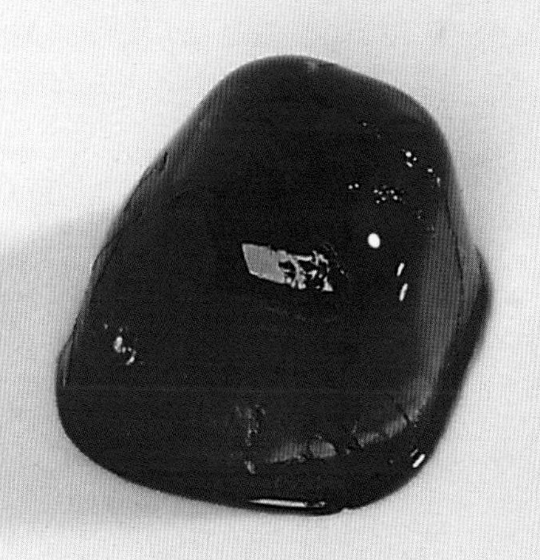

Look at the red ice cube.

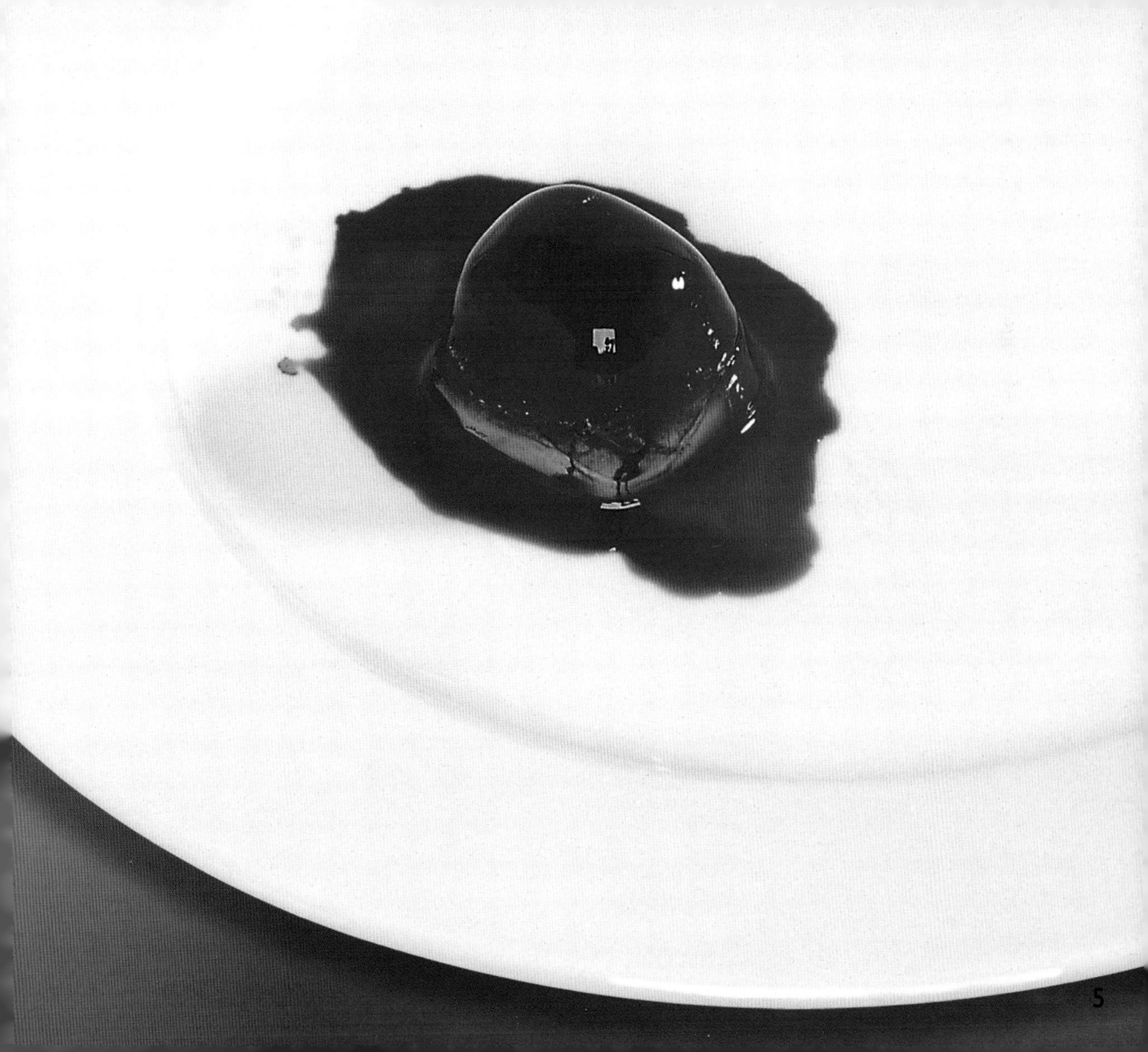

Here is a yellow ice cube.

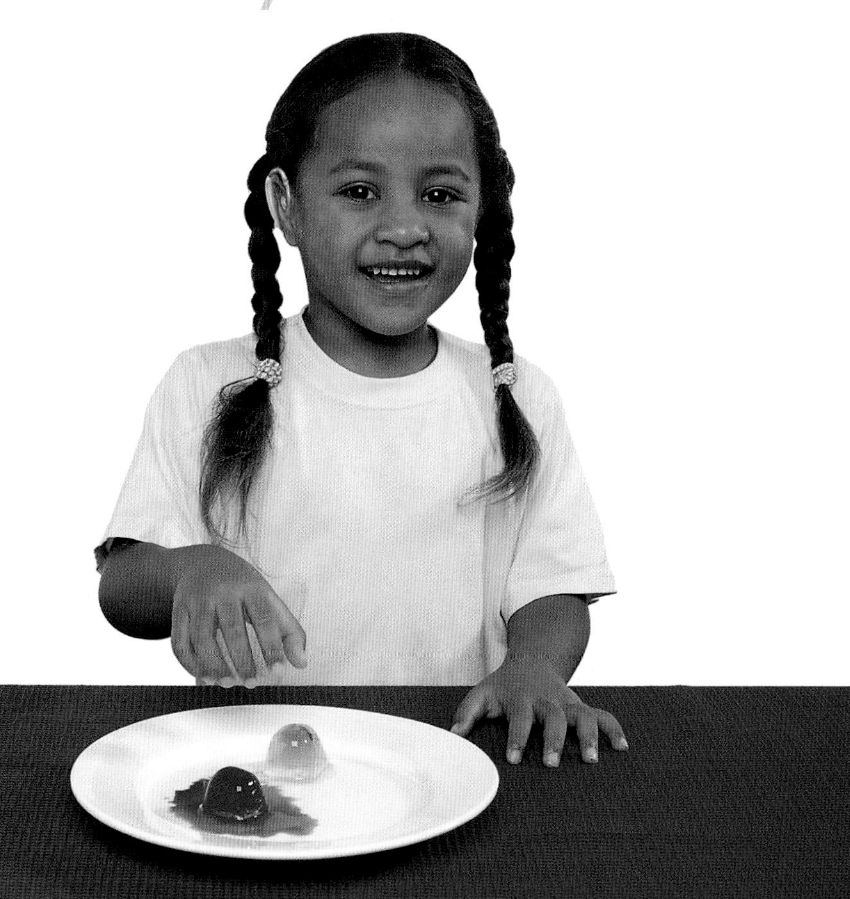

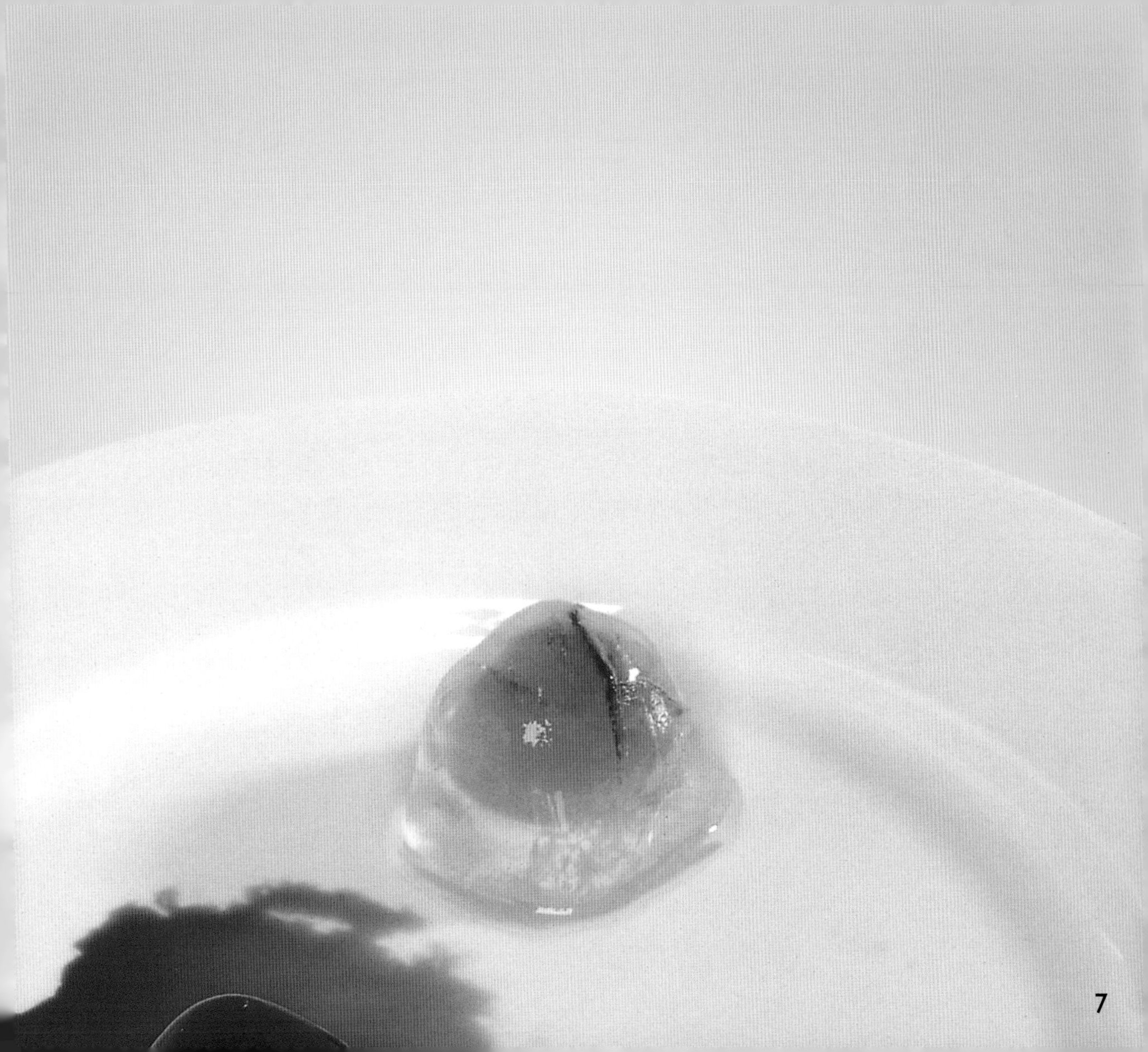

Look at the yellow ice cube.

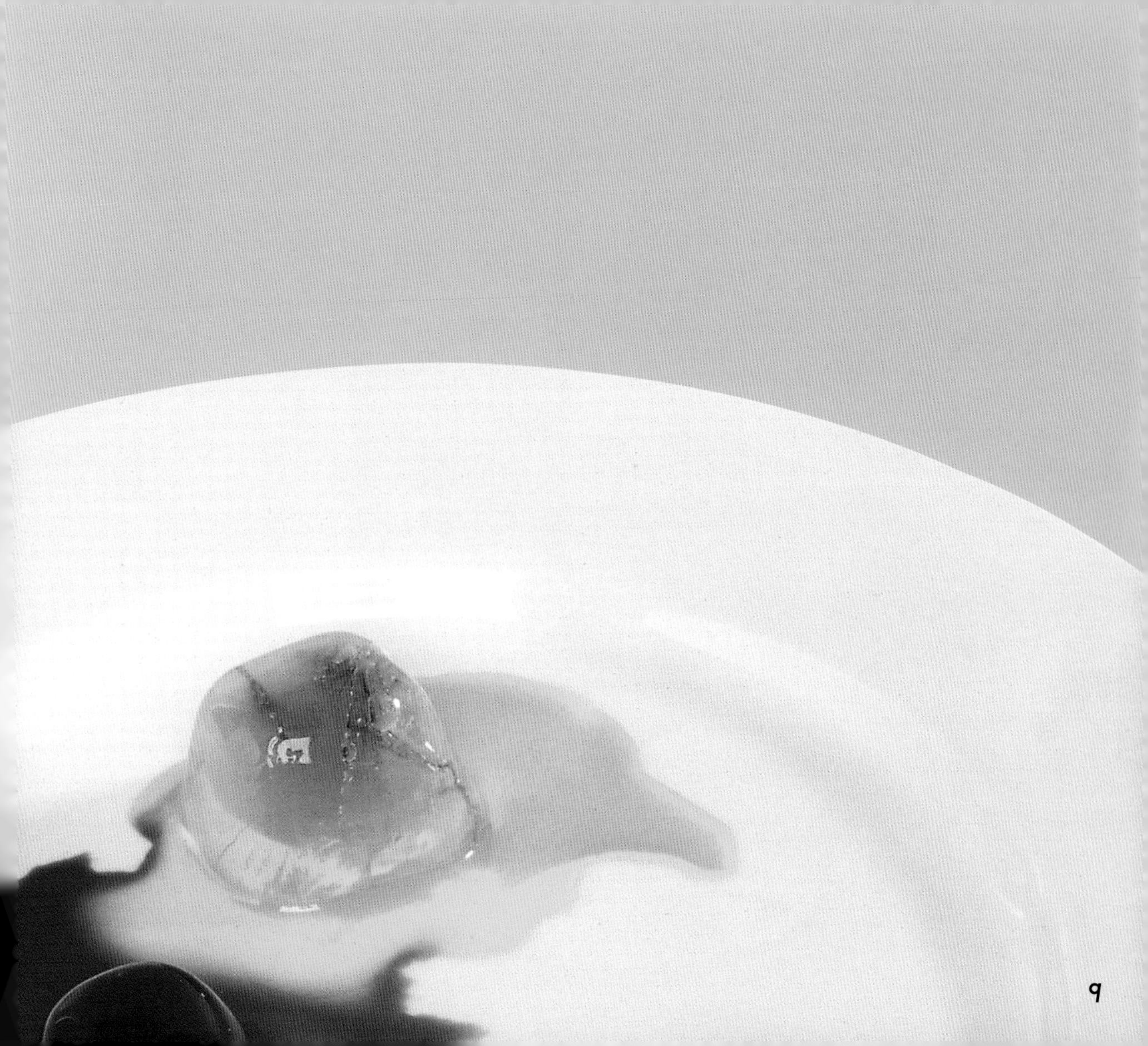

Here is a green ice cube.

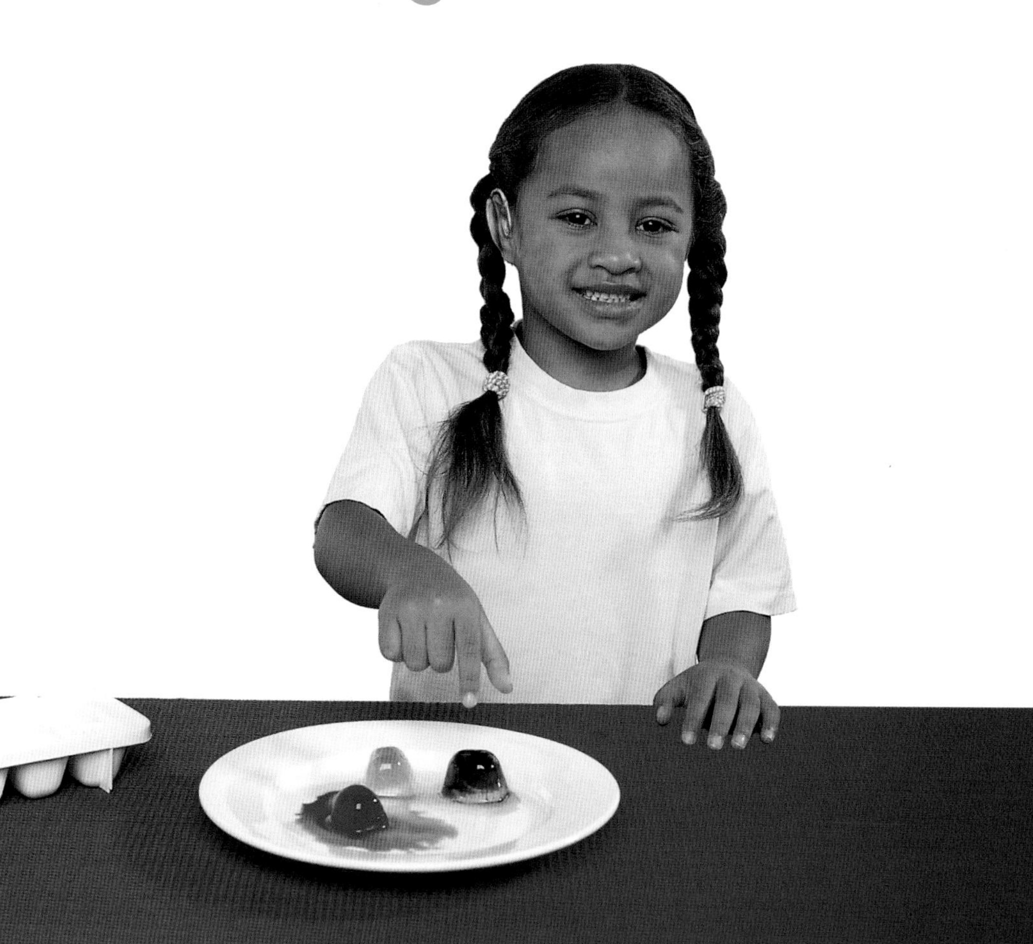

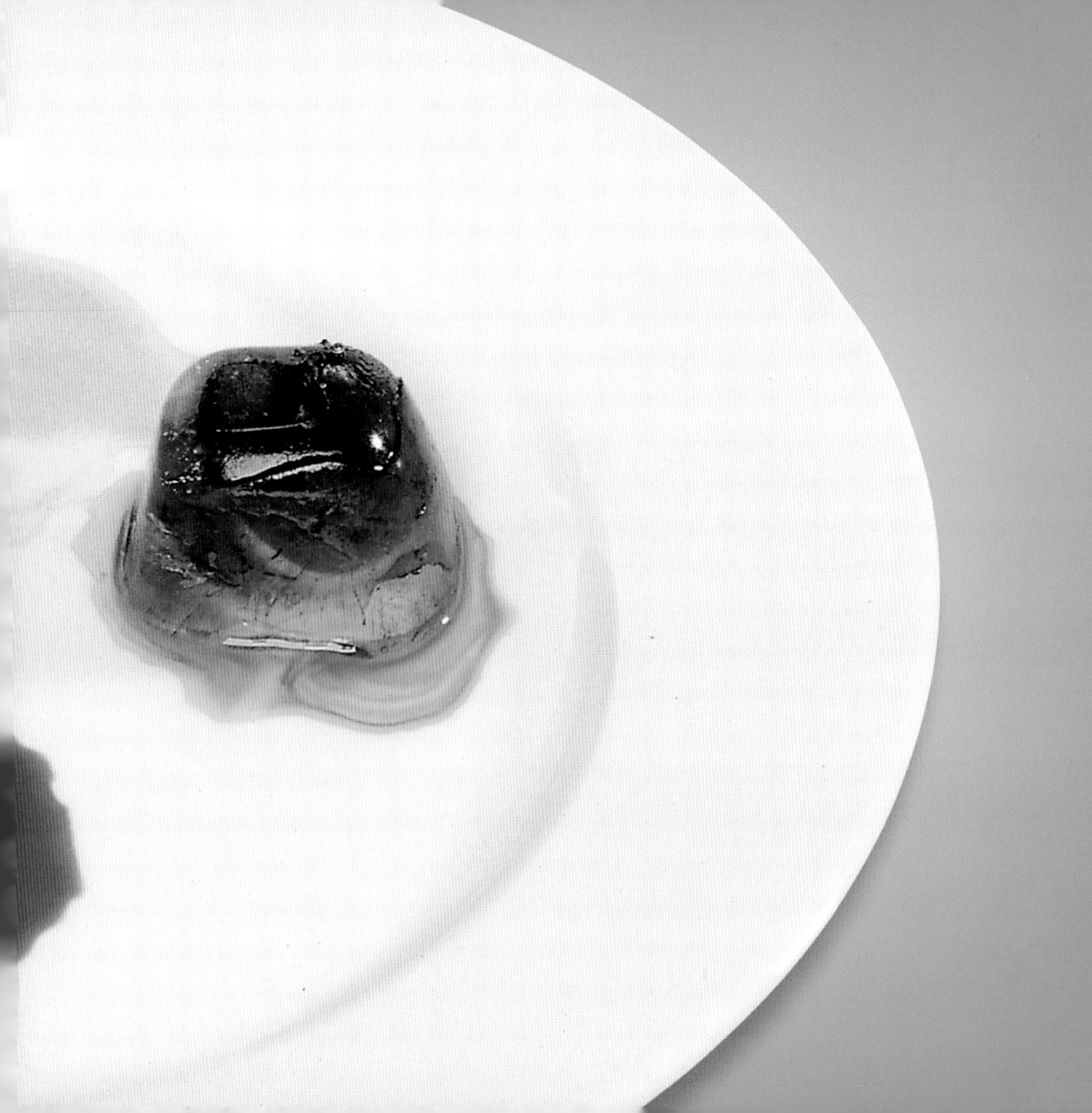

Look at the green ice cube.

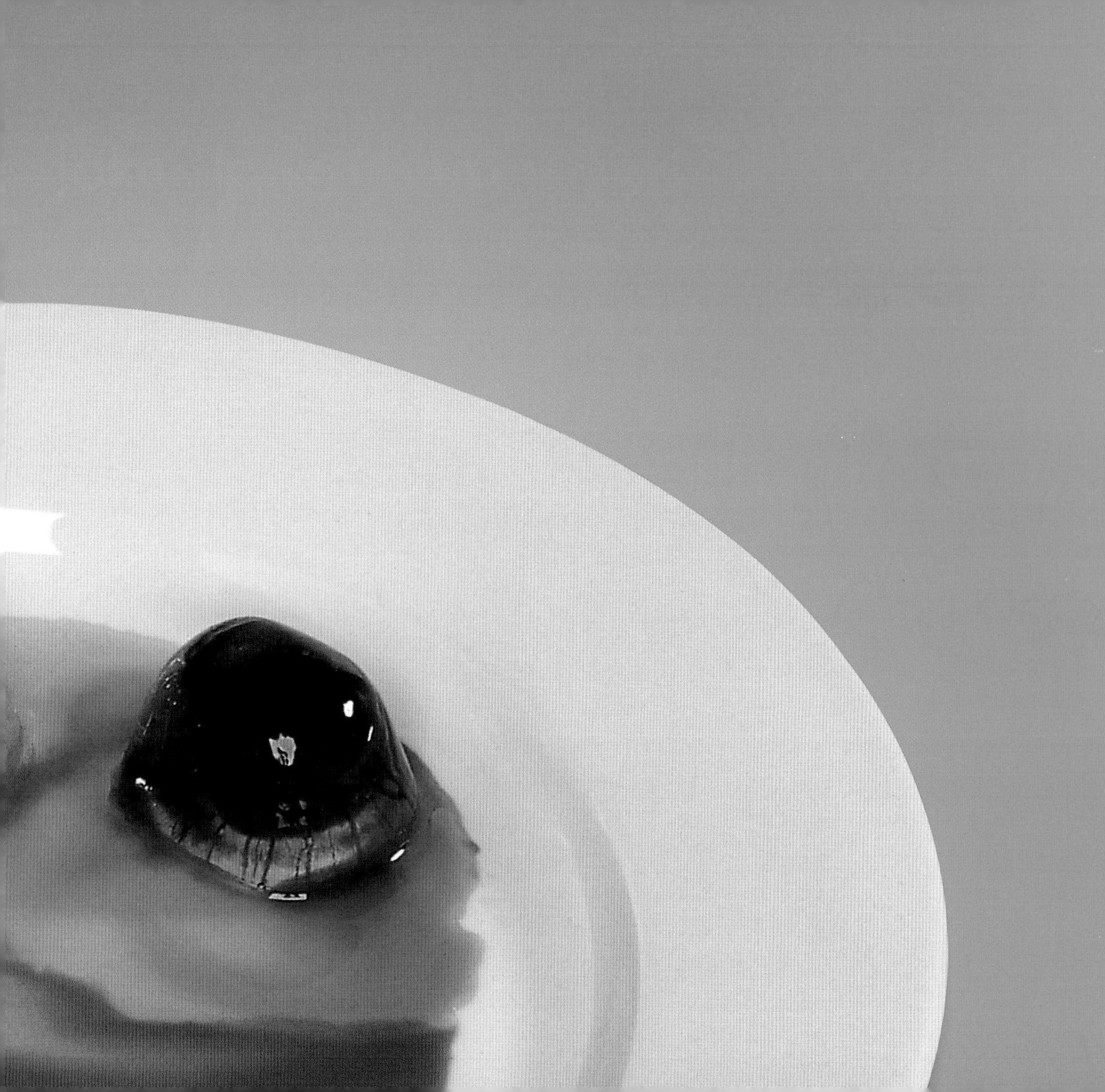

Look at the ice cubes.

The ice cubes

are melting.

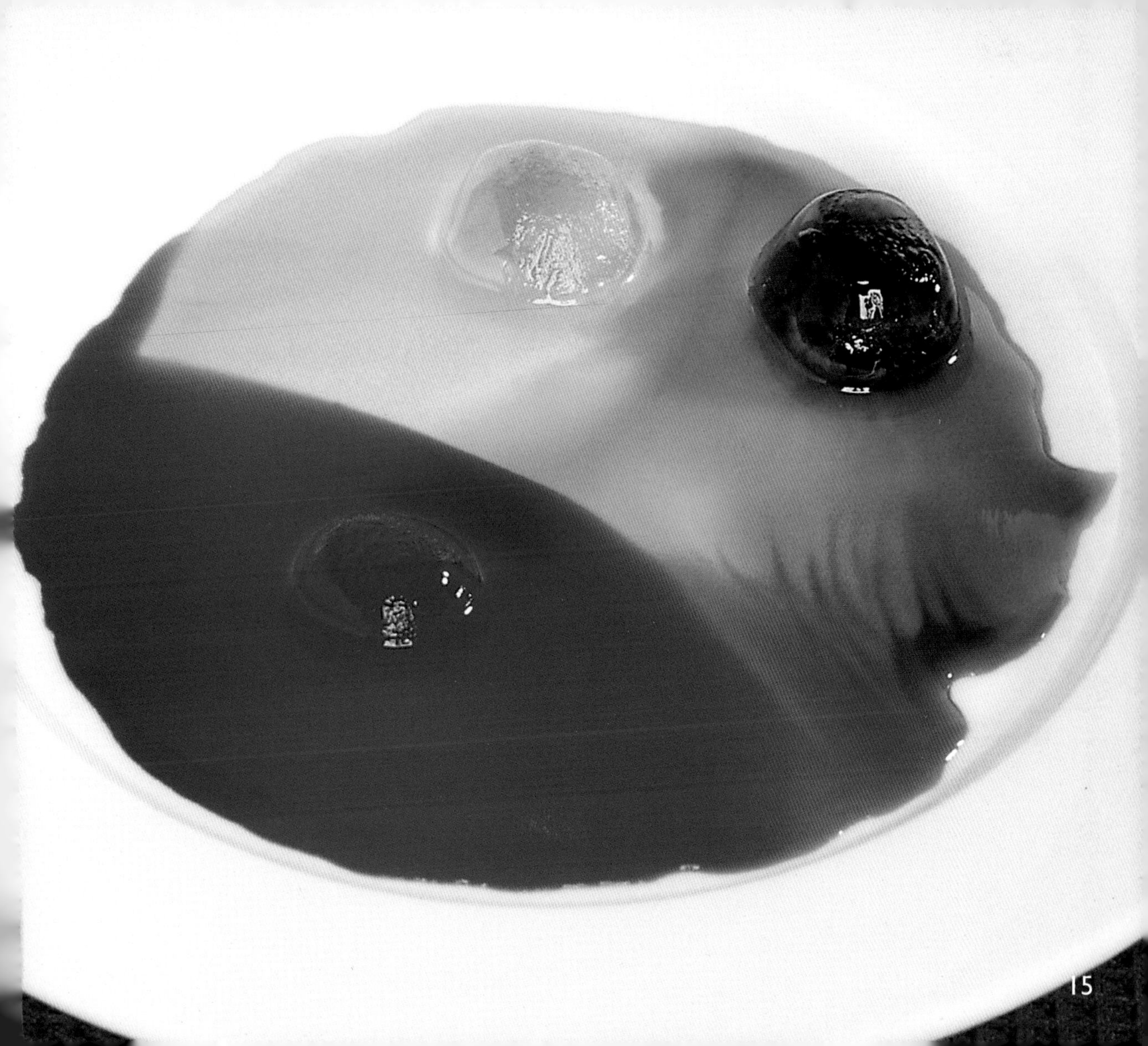

Look at the water.

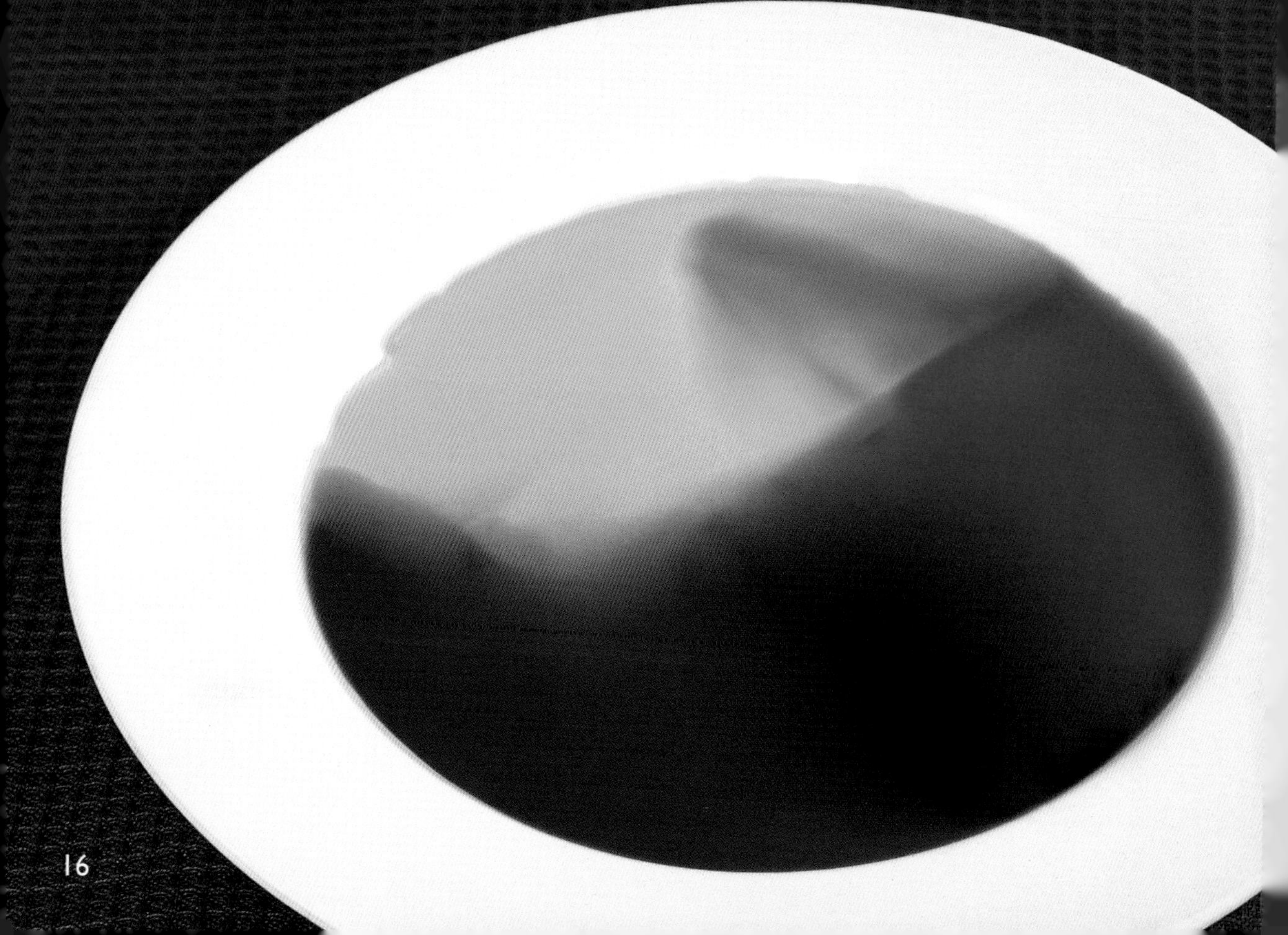